Snow Bunny's Christmas Wish

To Sharon, because you're a star!

Lots of love, Bek xxx

Snow Bunny's Christmas Wish was originally published in the United Kingdom by Nosy Crow Ltd. in 2012.

Library of Congress Cataloging-in-Publication Data Available

ISBN 978-0-545-55070-3

10 9 8 7 6 5 4 3 2 1   13 14 15 16 17

First American edition, September 2013

Printed in China

The text type was set in Bookman Old Style.

Snow Bunny's Christmas Wish

Rebecca Harry

Orchard Books

An Imprint of Scholastic Inc. • New York

Snow Bunny lived all by herself deep in the wintry forest.

Every day she hummed a happy song, but there was one thing she wished for more than anything.

On Christmas Eve, Snow Bunny decided to ask
Santa to make her wish come true.
So she wrote him a letter in her
best handwriting.

Dear Santa,
For Christmas please
may I have a friend?
This is the only
present I truly
want.
Thank you.
Snow Bunny
X X X

She addressed
the envelope carefully so it
wouldn't get lost in the mail,

and she hurried out
into the frosty air just in time . . .

. . . to see Red Robin Postman flying away.
She had missed him by a whisker.

"Oh, no!" said Snow Bunny. "I'll have to deliver my letter to Santa myself."

Snow Bunny looked at her map.

"I will follow the North Star to Santa's house," she said. "I won't get lost, but just in case, I'd better pack some useful things."

Wintry Forest

Frozen Pond

North Star

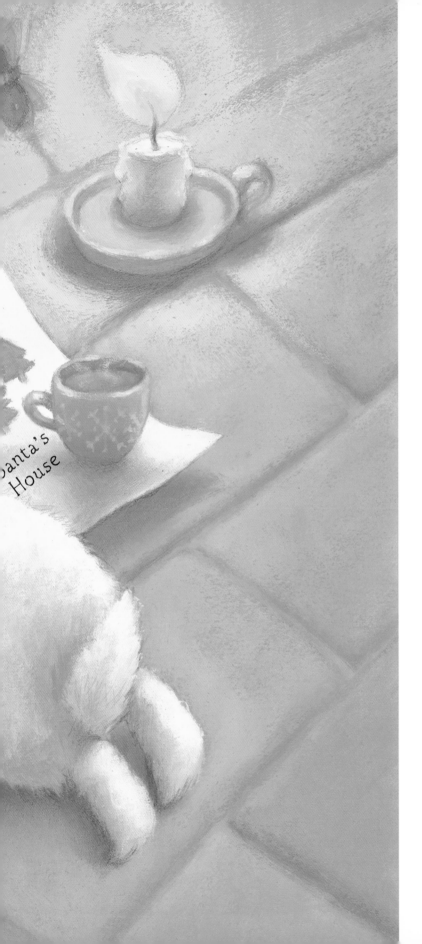

She packed a pair of warm
mittens . . .

. . . some frosted cookies . . .

. . . and her map.

Snow Bunny had been walking
through the snow for a little while when
she saw a light shimmering through the trees.

"There's the North Star!" she said happily.
But as she pushed through the trees, she saw . . .

. . . it was only the moon shining on a frozen pond.
Bears skated across the ice, all having fun . . .

. . . except one small cub,

who sat by himself
blowing on his cold,
cold paws.

Snow Bunny thought for a moment.
"You can have my mittens to keep
your paws warm," she said kindly,
and she went on her way.

She hadn't gone far
when she spotted a star
high above the trees.

"That must be the North Star!"
she said hopefully.
But as she came down the hill, she saw . . .

. . . it was the star on top of a huge Christmas tree.

Animals scampered around, hanging decorations from its pretty branches . . . all except one little fox cub, who had no decoration to add.

Snow Bunny thought for a moment.
"You can use my frosted cookies to
decorate the tree," she said
kindly to the fox cub . . .

. . . and she went on her way.

She had gone quite far when she saw a wavering light.
"Is that the North Star?" she wondered, but on the
other side of the hedge, she saw . . .

. . . the light was from the lanterns of some fawns, who had been out visiting friends and had lost their way.

Snow Bunny thought for
a moment.

"You can have my map so you can find
the path home," she said kindly.
And they went on their way.

Snow Bunny blew on her cold paws.
She felt hungry and a little bit lost.

Then she took one last
long look up at the sky, and
what did she see?

"That *must* be the North Star!" she
exclaimed. "It is so big and beautiful!"
And as she ran toward it, she saw . . .

. . . that it *was* the North Star, shining brightly over Santa's house!

Santa read Snow Bunny's letter.
"Hop on my sleigh. I'll take you home
on my way delivering presents
and making wishes come true
around the world."

"But what about my wish, Santa?"
Snow Bunny asked politely.

"Wait and see," smiled Santa, and with a "giddyup," they whooshed off through the dark and starry night.

When Santa's sleigh landed outside her home deep in the wintry forest, Snow Bunny saw all the animals she'd met along the way gathered at her door.

They had all come
to thank her for her help.

What a happy Christmas the new
best friends spent together!
Snow Bunny's Christmas
wish had come true.